T0121740

THE ROYAL SWINTONS
R/S

by
Tracie Walker

Order this book online at www.trafford.com
or email orders@trafford.com

Most Trafford titles are also available at major online book retailers.

© Copyright 2009 Tracie Walker
All rights reserved. No part of this publication may be reproduced, stored in a retrieval system, or
transmitted, in any form or by any means, electronic, mechanical, photocopying, recording, or
otherwise, without the written prior permission of the author.

Printed in Victoria, BC, Canada.

ISBN: 978-1-4269-1504-8

*Our mission is to efficiently provide the world's finest, most comprehensive book publishing
service, enabling every author to experience success. To find out how to publish your
book, your way, and have it available worldwide, visit us online at www.trafford.com*

Trafford rev. 1/29/2010

Cover design by Kat Pettaway

North America & international
toll-free: 1 888 232 4444 (USA & Canada)
phone: 250 383 6864 ♦ fax: 812 355 4082

THE ROYAL SWINTONS

R/S

Welcome

Narrator: *Hi, it's me. If you haven't guessed. I'm you're friendly neighborhood story teller with your friendly neighborhood story.*

This one's about a Surveyor for the crown and his name was William Swinton. He was a lonely man. A man with no direction, with no purpose. OK I listen to too much radio.

Anyway, he thought he was by himself in the world. Well he fell in love with this woman who turned out to be a member of the Royal family. She didn't marry him but by a far stretch of his imagination, in his mind, he became part of the Royal Community. He even dubbed himself a "Royal" Swinton. Give a man an inch, he'll take a mile.

Anyway, after some thorough investigation, he found out that there were more Swintons around the world. But they all knew they were put on this planet for some reason but couldn't quite put their fingers on it. They only knew that the were destined for something big. Well since William didn't see himself as a surveyor anymore but Royalty, he thought there had to be a way to find his family.

Then the strangest thing happened. With a little majic and a lot of imagination, he concocted a way to not only find the other Swintons but bring them to the Palace. But first he had to get one.

By 1730, he finished his Palace. Home Sweet Home. Then traveled all over the world. His zest for fame and fortune took him on an odyssey of trials and tribulations. Years had gone by and through both love and lust, he had two daughters, Sasha and Sizzli (pronounced sizzle). Although they were family, they were raised in two different corners of the world and it seems that trials and tribulations were inherited. Here's where the story really picks up. At least that's where I'm gonna start.

THE ROYAL SWINTONS
R/S
Index

THE ROYAL SWINTONS
R/S

CAST OF CHARACTERS

Sasha Swinton	Eccentric ex- millionairess who lost her fortune to love
Sizzli Swinton	Every day Jane type who always gets caught up in something
Mr. D.	Sasha's Limo Driver
Maid	Sasha's maid
Ganna Gain	Sizzli's best friend
Mr. Doorman	Works for Handy Dandy Diggs
MaeB	Owner - MaeB Babi Novelties
Mr. & Ms. Thang	Owners of The Others Night Club.
Bus Driver	For the Eastside Bus
Narrator	What do you think?

And starring

THE STRANGEST THING (Ah chew – I sneezed.)

THE ROYAL SWINTONS
R/S

Scene I

INTRODUCING SASHA SWINTON

Scene: *In a REALLY big mansion in a REALLY big city in the distance or should I say way way way in the distance lived Sasha Swinton.*

Scene: And there she is - standing in the foyer near the front door in front of or a REALLY big mirror tilting her head from side to side listening to the beads in her hair make that crackling sound.

Sasha was in her own world watching the beads hit one side of her scalp to the other singing, aaaand to the left side…ttthhheeenn to the right side… aaaand to the left side…ttthhheeenn to the right side… humpf

So there she stood in her REALLY colorful satin floral dress at the door with a REALLY tacky bag. From the looks of things, she REALLY should have gotten a better bag. She has plans to go on a REALLY great vacation - or so she thinks.

In the background is the maid rolling her REALLY plush wheel chair briskly down the hall to Sasha saying loudly in desperation,

Maid

Ma Lady. Ma Lady, you know you haven't paid me in two weeks.

I know you've been so busy. I'm sure it just slipped your mind and.......

Sasha (cuts her off. She put her bag down and pounds her hand on her waist and yells.)

You don't deserve any pay because you twisted my hair. humpf!!

Maid

But Ma Lady, They're **called** twists.

Sasha (*turns around, pointing her finger and says*) I don't care! YYOOOUUU did it. Now you - are - holding - me – up! I'm going on vacation. Humpf!! (*She grabs her bag with two hands and out the door, off to the limo she's headed.*)

> *Scene: The driver, Mr. D, opens the door with a snarl. Sasha lugging her bag with two hands and her head hung low because she knows that she hasn't paid him in two months. She trips and starts to fall. Good thing the limo was there to catch her fall.*

Narrator: *Why does Mr. D stay around? He has worked for her for years.--- That was --before she lost everything.*

Mr. D *(Says in a silent whisper while he's shaking his head walking to open the door for Sasha...)*

Now - I don't know about you, but when you have a thriving one-sided bread browning business like Sasha Swinton and get drunk with Teddy Toast, The King of The Metal Dispensers. You're bound to end up loosing everything. It was front-page news!

EXTRA – EXTRA – EXTRA   READ ALL ABOUT IT

SWINTON IS TOTALLY COOKED!!!!!

At the bottom of the page

COMING TO A STORE NEAR YOU - THE TOASTER!!!

(It darkens your bread on both sides)

Narrator: *He opens Sasha's door, she tosses her bag with two hands in and helps her into the car. Mr. D closes the door, looks back and says,*

Mr. D

You comfortable?

And heads to the drivers seat. Takes his seat, fastens the seat belt, puts the key in the ignition....

Mr. D *(cont.)*

Poor Sasha's acting like nobody knows. I've got love for her so I stick around. The only staff left is me and Mrs.C the cook. And if I'm not mistaken, I saw her going out the back with her bags. One day Sasha's going to loose me too.

Sasha *(with an attitude)*

Well Man, *(She thinks to herself - What is his name?)* It's really nice to share this time with you but I think if you could take this opportunity to turn the key, we might even **go somewhere!!!** Humpf

Mr. D.

Yes Ma Lady. You know what? I saw The Strangest Thing! AhChew (He sneezed). Well never mind. I'm sorry… Ma Lady, what's the destination?

Sasha

Look, you've taken me to the same places ALLLL the time. You know that I'm goin on vacation. If you don't know by now where **I** wanna go *(like a child)* I'm not gonna let you take me aaannnnyyywwwhhheeerrr **again.. SOOOOO MOVE!!!** I always have to tell you where to take me. Allll the time. Allll the time. humpf

Mr. D.

Well I'll tell you where you're **not** going to take **me EVA EVA AGAIN** - anymore too. It's been….. Good day Ma Lady!!!

Narrator: *And he gets out of the limo, slams the door and starts walking away. He turns to look back and sees Sasha getting out on the other side yelling in languages that he had never heard --- loudly. They make eye contact and from the expression he saw on her face and her hair standing on end with all those boretts, and fire around her head, he turns around and starts hauling as fast as he could to somebody's car at the other side of the drive way. He gets in and squeals down the driveway burning rubber the whole way.*

Back to Sasha

(She yells,)   Man! Man!

(frustrated)   What **is** his **name**???

(She yells,)   Man!

(with a wimper)   Come Back Man! I can't believe this!

(She yells,)   Lady!

(frustrated again) What is **her name**???

(She starts yelling to the maid).   Laaady!

   She walks back up to the house. Puts the key in the lock. Turns it and the key breaks off in her hand.

Sasha

Oh nao! What else??

Narrator: *Sometimes there are questions that you really shouldn't ask.*

Sasha happens to turn around and sees Lady in her wheel chair with bags packed on a rack in the back - rollin.......

Lady *(Yelling)*

It's been..... Good day Ma Lady – and pulls back the throttle, tosses back her head cracking up as she rolls off into the sunset.

Sasha *(Yelling in the air).*

That's alright! I've got the keys to the limo. So how you like me now!!! Humpf!

She gets in the drivers seat, props herself up like she's so sure - so confident. She turns on the radio, and the song is playing by Earth Wind and Fire– AIN'T NO STOPIN US NOW. She grabs the rear view mirror to adjust it. In amazement, she sees just how BIG that limo is.

Sasha

I've never seen it from up front. Humpf.

So there she is, looking in the rear view mirror, tosses her hair from left to right singing aaaand to the left side...ttthhheeenn to the right side. Then she pauses and says:

Oh man!. *(with a child's squeal)* Mommy, I'm not in the Benz anymore.

Narrator: What she does see WAAAAAAY to the rear window ledge was something that looked like a medallion. Her eyes get big as saucers. Then she pauses, again

Sasha

Wait a minute *(excitedly)* UUUUHHH!! What have we here? I'll bet it's diiiiamonds. TT wouldn't really leave me with nothing. I'll bet it's a locket with a ticket for me to meet him somewhere. humpf

She's so excited, she climbs through the privacy window across the seat through the body of the limo tearing pieces of her satin dress along the way. Knocking over glasses on the island bar. Tearing the curtains and finally she makes it to the back of the limo.

Sasha

I made it TT. I'll be right there. I know….. you miss me.

She sees the golden medallion with R/S in the center. Under it was a note. She picked up the medallion and it shattered but the pieces faded away.

Narrator: She was confused but wanted to read the note – From

TT or so she thought. They say no news is good news – well it all depends on how you look at it.

The note read: you think you have it all - you don't.
you think you don't have a thing - you do.
*Look for **the others** and you'll find - what's yours*
Go to the Eastside and you'll get - a clue. A Palace awaits

Narrator: *That's what she needs to get – a clue*

Sasha

Oh great. Riddles. I still don't know which came first. The chicken or the egg? The only thing I understood is go to the Eastside. Well, I guess my Benz is out, Ms. C took that. Lady took the wheel chair and I can't even get Man to walk with me. Oh yeeah! I've got a liiimozeene. *(like a bratt)* I GOT A LIIIMO! I GOT A LIIIMO!

She opens the door and steps out. Turns around and closes the door like a limo driver and snickers.

Sasha *(looking back at the door)*

She gets back in the drivers seat. I'm comfy? Humpf! I've fastened my seat belt. Looks in the rear view and starts crying like I Love Lucy: **AAAAAHHHH- HAAAAAAA - I GOT A LLLIIIMMMOOO!!!**

THE ROYAL SWINTONS
R/S

Scene II

INTRODUCING SIZZLI SWINTON

Scene: In the middle of a small town in a small apartment I say really really, really small. More like a human roach motel, but they can come out - lives Sizzli Swinton.

There, in the kitchen stands Sizzli. She's got on her maids uniform preparing for her day job. Holding a bowel in one hand and a box of Goast Toasties in the other and a can of evaporated milk on the counter. Singing.

Sizzli

I'm Sizzli. I'm lean. I'm Sizzli. I'm lean. Wait a minute, does that make me Sizzli lean? Ha! **(she chuckles).** Oh boy my bestest breakfast. Ghost Toasties and Evaporated Milk mmm mmm mmm mmm toastie!

She pours the Toasties and milk into the bowl, digs the spoon in and heads to the "squat" room.

Narrator: I did say this is a really really small apartment – just enough room to squat. Just as Sizzli goes to take a squat, in walks here best friend in the whole wide world Ganna Gain. The only thing **she'll** *gain - is weight. She had trecked up the steps and   carefully navigated her way through the door of Sizzli's apartment.*

Ganna

I don't know about you Sizzli girl. You work two jobs and always caught up in something. You can't seem to keep money. The only green around here is in the refrigerator. It's a good thing that this building is all inclusive.

What it **should** include is… **(she looks around) SOME SPACE!!!**

Sizzli

Hey girl. Ganna Gain! Gain any good news?   No? Gain any bad news?   No? Gain any more weight? – ha ha **(she looks at Ganna and nods)**YEEPPPP!

Ganna

Girl stop. You know I'm still as fine as ever. Don't sweat the small stuff.

Sizzli

You need to sweat cause you ain't small stuff.

(Both girls laughed)

Sizzli

If **you** were small stuff, I could get you a job with me at that new club THE OTHERS.

Ganna

The Others? Girl you know that I won't get naked in front of anybody.

Narrator: *You think?*

Sizzli

I'm an exotic dancer Ganna. I **do** wear shorts and a top. And you know it's only for the money. Something's gonna change Ganna. I feel it. Besides nobody in their left mind would want to see AAALLLL that in a pair of shorts!

Ganna

Whatever!!! You know, I saw The Strangest Thing - AhChew *(She sneezed)* on my way over here. I've lived in this spit of a town all my life and I've never ever seen anything like it.

Sizzli

Bless you. Like what?

Ganna

The Strangest Thing. AhChew. *(She sneezed)*

Sizzli

Bless you. Girl - What was it?!

Ganna

Sizzli. You don't hear so good. **I SAID THE STRANGEST THING!!** AhChew (She sneezed)

Come on I'll introduce you.

Narrator: *As painful as it must have been, Ganna carefully navigated herself back through the door of Sizzli's apartment and trecked back down the steps with Sizzli right behind ALLL of her.*

Sizzli (as they walk down the steps and out of the building)

That's a NAME?

Ganna

Yea girl. I'm trying to tell you….The Strangest Thing AhChew (She sneezed)

Sizzli

Bless you. Oh wait a minute, I forgot the trash. I'll be right back. Wait right here. Don't run away…….haaa

Ganna

You're lucky I like you – some. Just hurry up!!!

Narrator: *Sizzli runs back into the apartment. She goes to retrieve the little trash she had accumulated and back downstairs she had business. Ganna was pacing back and forth. After a minute Sizzli returns.*

Sizzli

Ganna, I'm back now where is this Strangest Thing?

Ganna

It's **The** Strangest Thing AhChew (She sneezed). It was right here a minute ago. I smiled, it smiled and.........

Sizzli

What do you mean **it**? First you say the strangest thing and then you say ...**it**. Girl are you alright? Change your medication? Now you're making me late for work. Sometimes I wonder about you Ganna. Go get some sleep or some fries or something. Ganna **go!!!!**

Ganna

I'm telling you. I saw The Strangest Thing AhChew (She sneezed). We've been friends for how long Sizzli Swinton? Have I ever lied to you?

Sizzli

Bless you. Lied? No! Embellished a little - well yeah. You used to tease me about my last name. Remember? Why did the chicken cross the road? To get to the Swinton side. That wasn't funny. What does a carpenter do? Swin-a-ton-na-bricks? Again - not funny.

One day I'll show you what a Swinton really is. Now I'm late. If I hurry, I'll keep my day job.

Narrator: *With the bag of trash Sizzli goes to the back to the trash cans. She tosses her bag in the can, turns around and out of the corner of her eye, she sees the golden medallion with* R/S *in the center. Under it was a note. She picked up the medallion and it shattered but the pieces faded away. She was confused but wanted to read the note.*

The note read: *You think you don't have a thing - you do.*
You want to have it all - you will.
The others *will help you to find - what's yours*
You'll know what to do when you pay the bill.
A Palace awaits

Sizzli

OK? What's this about? I work at The Others. A bunch of crazies. All these guys want to do is stick to you like glue.

She put the note in her pocket.

Narrator: *So off to her day job Sizzli goes at Handy Dandy Diggs. She's a cleaning lady, or as they say at the Handy Dandy, a Dirt Specialist. As she looks both ways and starts crossing the street, she almost gets run over by this grey limousine. The lady driving like a bat out of - someplace hot. It's Sasha. Sasha looks out the window at Sizzli. Sizzli who can read the words coming out of her mouth........*

Sasha

MORON!!! Humpf

Sizzli (yelling)

If that car is too big, get a Benz!!! Yeah right. A Benz. Haaa What was her hurry? I'm the one that's gonna be late.

Narrator: Well Sizzli has had her startle for this morning. Now she's going to the one place that she can count on for money – Handy Dandy Diggs.

Mr. Doorman

Hey there Ms. Sizzli. Whatcha know? Looking good today, as always.

Sizzli

Thanks Mr. Dee. It's been an interesting few hours. I went from my favorite breakfast to some Strangest Thing. Now I guess it'll be alright today.

Mr. Doorman

You know what Sizzli, I know you have another job but you are aces with me. I only hear good things about you from the guests and even the Management. You're in for some good money. *(he says as he's rubbing his fingers against his thumb).* You keep up the good work child.

Sizzli

Well thank you Mr. Dee. You're a good man.

Mr. Doorman

Did you say The Strangest Thing? AhChew (He sneezed)

Sizzli

Bless you. Everybody must be catching a cold. Yeah that's right. The Strangest Thing. My friend Ganna says she saw **it**. Do you know what **it** is Mr. Dee?

Mr. Doorman

I know that strange things happen. My cousin did some strange things. There was this time…….

Sizzli

That's ok Mr. Dee. I've got work to do. Bye now.

Narrator: So now Sizzli has gone to the closet to retrieve her bucket. She takes out the note and reads it again.

> *you think you don't have a thing - you do.*
> *you want to have it all - you will.*
> ***the others** will help you to find - what's yours*
> *You'll know what to do when you pay the bill. A Palace awaits*

Well the day's work is done. It was amazingly slow today. Mr. Doorman catches her before she leaves.

Mr. Doorman

Sizzli, Mr. Bossman gave me your check to give to you. Can I have it?

Sizzli

Go head Mr. Dee. Thank you. When I get rich, you can have it. My check that is…… I won't need it.

Mr. Doorman

OK. You be careful out there. Don't take any wooden nickels. What the heck are nickels???

Off Sizzli goes back to the "Motel" to change her clothes.

THE ROYAL SWINTONS
R/S

Scene III

Sasha finds The Others

Scene: Back to Sasha
She's frustrated because she can't find anywhere to park this really big car. She finally finds a space that's not quite big enough.

Sasha

I really wish that I cold find a parking space or make this bigger.

Narrator: Suddenly, her left shoulder starts to itch. She reaches with her right hand to scratch it and like magic, the cars seemed to move. The space opened really wide. Enough to fit two limos.

Sasha

Woah! I thought that spot was too small. WHA - HAPPEN? No matter. *(Like a child)* I got a paaaarking space! I got a paaaarking space!

Narrator: I guess it would have been a good thing if Sasha could park. After umpteen tries. The car is finally in the space. The telephone pole was ruined but she's in.

Across the street was an interesting place. The sign reads:

MayBe Babi.
The store for those that just don't quite know.

Sasha grabs her bag with two hands and lugs it to the shop.

Sasha

Hello there. *(she says with much unnecessary pride)* **MY** name Sasha. I'm looking for a room. I'll need a place with a safe. I've got all my diamonds and furs and cash bonds in a case that need to be locked up. Is there anywhere in this spit of a town that can accommodate me? Humpf

Narrator: Now how on this planet should she think anybody will actually take her seriously. Her dress is ripped, her hair is missing a few borets and that's not the only thing that's missing from her head. Know what I mean? Plus she looks like she'd definitely seen better days. - Maybe.

MaeB *(looking confused)*

Well hi there. I'm Mae. You wanna know if we've got rooms? Well maybe. Ha ha I love sayin that. Need a room? You don't look like you fit in round here. What brings you to this Neck.

Narrator: She didn't mean neck of the woods either. Remember this is a small city and the corner shops are on the street called Neck. I guess I should warn you that there are 4 streets called Neck. Somebody came up with that bright idea. It's the law. You just can't break it.

Sasha

I just need a place. I need a place **NOW**. *(And then, as if she were catching herself.)* I'm an entertainment inspector and I need to know where do you people go for entertainment? I've got places to go and people to see. *humpf*

MaeB

Well shugga, there's the Muddled Mass and the Doubting Thomas. That's just on these streets. And on the others..... Nodda Chance and Ahh Maaan.

Narrator: OK don't ask. I didn't name them either.

Sasha

Wait!

*Narrator: Her eyes get wide with excitement because all Sasha heard was **the others** and she takes out the note:*

> *you think you have it all - you don't.*
> *you think you don't have a thing - you do.*
> *Look for **the others** and you'll find - what's yours*
> *Go to the Eastside and you'll get - a clue. A Palace awaits*

Sasha *(cont.)*

The note said the others so….

Narrator: She picks up her bag with two hands and sprints to the limo. Now here goes the unpark wiggle. Poor telephone poll.

THE ROYAL SWINTONS
R/S

Scene IV

Welcome to The Others

Scene: Now back at the "Motel" Sizzli is trying to find her "other" work clothes. She thinks about the day's events. Since the room isn't big enough for a proper shower. We'll just call it a large human wet bar. Sizzli takes a shower, looks at the clock and is late - again. She's supposed to be at work at 9 and it's now 9:45.

Sizzli

DOOOGGG! I wish I could be just a little early just once in my life.

Narrator: Then Sizzli's left shoulder started itching so she scratches. Running like she was doing a marathon, she runs two blocks to The Others. When she gets there, she runs straight past one of the owner, Ms. Thang, to the changing room. Picks up her time card, puts it in the time box. It gets stamped with the "Time In". When she looks at it, it reads 8:55.

Sizzli

Well I've got to get a new battery for that clock. Hey Ms. Thang. Think it'll be busy tonight?

Ms. Thang

Well girl, I j j jus don't know. We put out the fl fl fl fl - uuuh fl fl fl fl - uh that paper with our name onnum. All over the place.

Narrator: OK four pieces of paper. One per neck.

Sizzli

I hear we've got new meat today.

Narrator: Think about it...

Sizzli

That hamburger was a waist of a bun. I sort of grows on you though. Well it's not growing like that stuff in my refrigerator. Well since I'm here early, I guess I can start setting up.

Narrator: Waite a minute. Sizzli's cleans for a living. What's up with her refrigerator? Let me tell you that this is a "family run" operation so in walks Mr. Thang. Not really the most pleasant man.

Mr. Thang

Hey there Sizzli. You got another new trick for these "customers"? That one you did last week was C R A Z Y!! How'd you do that?

Sizzli

Mr. Thang. come onnnn. That's the newest concept to please these customers. It's called a smile. You ought to try it sometime. It's a good thang Mr. Thang – ha ha ha ha.

Mr. Thang, you and Ms. Thang should take a vacation.

Mr. Thang

What, to hang with the Muddled Mass or the Doubting Thomas. Don't think so. That's alright. Ms. Thang wanted to go somewhere else but Nodda Chance and Ahh Maaan were booked solid.

Sizzli

You will be aaaalright Mr. Thang

THE ROYAL SWINTONS
R/S

Scene V

Sasha and Sizzli meet…

Narrator: Anyway, outside is a really frustrated Sasha. She's been all around this spit of a town North side, South side, West side, going almost full circle trying to get to the others. She's finally at the East Side. At least there's place to park this time, at the local airport. Right on the landing strip is one big plane and --- THE LIIMMOO.

She gets out – again – shuts the door – again. Goes to the back of the limo – again and grabs her big bag with two hands – again.

Sasha *(really, really frustated)*

Ask me where I'm goin'? I don't noooo. I just need to get to the other side. The other side. Doggon note!!! **Humpf!**

Narrator: Just when Sasha had had enough. There's a bus coming down the street. At the top, the sign reads – EAST SIDE. She sees the bus, starts kicking her bag and throws up her hand like a maniac trying to get the bus to stop.

Sasha

STOP!!! STOPPPPPP!! Do you **know** who I am?
Humpf!

Narrator: The bus driver see's this mad woman flailing her arms like she's about to take off. He see's that she must have been in a fight with somebody or something with her clothes all torn up. He's a little worried that this lady could be…well he's seen more stuff than enough but there won't be another bus for an hour so he stops, and she gets on.

Sasha *(gasping for air)*

Look, this town is so small but I seem to be going around in circles. I think I've been all over this side, can you **PLEASE** tell me how to get to The Others. humpf

Bus Driver

Sure Ms. *(he looks at that really big bag that she was kicking)* What's up with that dress and such a big bag? Going someplace?

Sasha

No. I just thought I'd make a **fashion statement.** Just drive! humpf

Narrator: Sasha pulls her big, tacky bag onto the bus. Since nobody was willing to help some crazy looking stranger she had to pull it on the bus herself. Oh the tragedy. Funny though. You see the look on

her fact??? She finally gets the bag on had taken a seat. Sweating and panting....

(Bus Driver drives for about 2 minutes)

Bus Driver

Ok Ms. This is your stop....

Sasha

You've got to be **kidding!** This is the other side????
humpf

Bus Driver

It's where you wanted to go isn't it? See that building *(says with much sarcasm)* with the big red, black and green sign that says **THE OTHERS**??? Come on, say it with me. Now get off of **my** bus.

Sasha *(dragging the bag off the bus - grumbling)*

Where is Man when I need him? This town is sooooo small - and that building? What's that all about? humpf

Narrator: Now here's the tricky part. Sasha has the greeaaatt big tacky bag trying to squeeze into the door to the Other Side. Sizzli is in the back stocking the sodas and sees this lady in a worn dress and borets justa hangin, dragging this really big, tacky bag and trying to squeeze into the door way. Sizzli's first thought was Ganna. That thought made her chuckle.

Sasha

Oh so you think this is funny do you? IT AIN'T FUNNY. Not as funny as **YOU** working in a dump like this. humpf

Sizzli

Yeah! Well! It may be a dump, but it's **my** dump!! Look, I'm sorry, you look like you could use some help.

Narrator: *That's an understatement.*

Sasha

I'm glad you noticed. **Can I get a hand here? humpf**

Sizzli

Look lady, I've got enough drama of my own, I don't need yours. If you want my help say PLEASE!!!

Sasha

Say **WHAT!!! PLEASE!!!** What do I look like to you? Do **you** know who **I** am??? humpf

Sizzli

From the looks of things, you look like you're the lady that needs some help. I could be wrong. Now who are you??

Sasha

Standing proud and confident. Throwing her shoulders back. I'm Sasha. Sasha Swinton and.......

Sizzli (interupts)

Sasha Swinton, *(smacking her forehead)* OH NO you've got to be kidding?

Narrator: She remembers the note: "the others will help you to find - what's yours". First thought - A Palace! FOR REAL? Next thought - I can handle this.

Sizzli (cont.)

Look, I'm sorry. I've had a - shall I say, very interesting day. Come on. I'll help you with that bag. *(Sizzli grabs one end and Sasha, the other)* What's in this thing? Looks like you're on a mission.

Sasha

You got that right. What a day. What a **day**. First - my husband......

Narrator: Sasha remembers that no body knows who she really is and if they do, they'll remember her as a wealthy woman whose broke as a joke. (ok just thought I'd slip that one in there) so she can't tell Sizzli her true story – yet....

Sasha *(cont.)*

Oh never mind. I don't know you and you don't know me. Let's keep it like that. Humpf

Sizzli

Girl, you've got a REAL attitude. Let's see what we can do about that. OK?

Sasha

Whatever!!! I usually get my maid to bring me dinner. Got **anything** around here to eat? humpf

Sizzli

Well we've got crackers and juice. Have some?

Sasha

You know if my stomach wasn't sounding off like an army battalion I'd say no but it doesn't look like I have a choice. I'll have some Ritzzy crackers and M'apple juice. I only **consume** the best. I deserve it. humpf

Sizzli

Tell you what. We've got smalteen crackers and prune juice. Whatchu gon do?

Sasha

Whatever!!!

Sizzli

Your dress – it's ......pretty.

Narrator: Now we all know she didn't mean that. Pretty what is the question.

Sizzli (cont.)

Looks warn - I mean warm. I happen to have a change of clothes in the back room. How bout we get you changed up? You look like my size.

Sasha

I don't do rayon. I definitely don't do polyester. I wear Japanese silk flown in all the way from China in the summer and delivered to me PERSONALLY by my Pilot; Indonesian satins shipped to me in the fall **uh** delivered to me by my Captain; The finest Mink Stoles, jackets AAANNNND coats in Winter and I don't even believe in cruelty to animals! EEEEVVVEN the aaabsolute best US hand woven cotton - woven by real people - in the fall. humpf

Sizzli

Looks more like a fanatical cat in the hat from the Caribbean hood delivered by YOOOOO ma ma. Look I don't have all that but I do have something. You think you can climb down off your high horse long enough to at least try them on. Go ahead. Make my day.

Sasha *(tired and drained from the day)*

MY horses are NOT on drugs. Besides I wouldn't bring them to a place like this anyway. There's no grass.

Narrator: *She didn't really say that did she? Yeah I guess she did.*

Sasha (cont.)

I have a limousine. But you wouldn't know anything about that. LOOK. I'm tired. I think I'm supposed to say something like **(It's a hard thing for Sasha to say)** TH TH TH Thanks. Humpf

Sizzli

No that ain't what you're supposed to be saaaying.

Sasha

ALRIGHT!!! **(in a tiny voice)** please

Sizzli

That'll have to do.

THE ROYAL SWINTONS
R/S

Scene VI

And Now - The Strangest Thing
Ah-Chew (I sneezed)

Narrator: They go into the little dressing room. There's a few little lockers a little bench little mirror and that's it.

Sizzli

OK. That bag is gonna have to stay right here. Don't worry, nobody will take it. They can't. It's WAAAY to big for any smart person to be bothered with. Plus it's tacky.

Sasha

TACKY!! TACKY!! What do you mean TACKY! This came in all the way from Milan. It's an original by Bill Baggins.

Sizzli

Well I don't care, it's tacky. T. A. C. K. Y. Tacky.

Sasha

Yeah! Well you're really dumba. D.U.M.ba. Nevermind. humpf

Narrator: *She goes to her really tacky bag and starts pulling out stuff . Objects are flying. Shoes, wigs, a hair dryer, an iron, a lamp, a spare tire, a bubble gum machine, and finally another dress.*

Sizzli

Shucks, looks like you have everything in there but the kitchen sick.

Sasha

I did but I changed bags. I left it in my other bag. Humpf

Sizzli

Holly mallolie girl.....

(Sasha struggles to pull that torn dress over her head)

Sasha

UUMMFFF UUUMMMFFF. One more time UUUMMMFFF!!!!

Sizzli (thinking)

Should I tell her that she has a zipper in the back – NAAAAHHH!!!

Sasha

OK – A little help here please.

Sizzli

Wow, I get "please" twice for a royal pain in my rucktuckus.

Narrator: She helped Sasha un zip the dress to pull it back over her head.   As the dress drops to the floor. Sizzli sees what she thinks is a tattoo.

Sizzli (cont.)

Cool tattoo Sasha. I've never seen anything like that round here. Who did it for ya Mr Needlz?

Sasha

Mr. Who?

Sizzli

No not Mr. Who - Mr Needlz the tattoo man.

Sasha

I'd never destroy my body with any tattoo's I'm not crazy. humpf

Narrator: Well, the jury's till out on that.

Sizzli

There it is right there on your left shoulder. See look. It's really nice. Whoever did it did a great job.

(She turns Sasha around so she can look over her shoulder to get a view in the mirror. What they see is R/S**)**

Sasha

Where did that come from. I've never seen it before and I should know. Humpf That's really something special.

Sizzli

You sure you didn't have it wished in all the way from Portugal and delivered directly from your Tooth Fairy? It really is a good one. Now that you've found something to wear, I have to change my clothes since you and your dirty, tacky bag got me all messed up. My customers don't want to see me all messed up.

Narrator: So now Sizzli has to change her clothes. Fortunately whatever she was going to let Sasha borrow is what she will have to change into. So Sizzli proceeds to remove her blouse and on her left shoulder is the same tattoo. The plot thickens...

Sasha

WHOOAAAA! You've got one too. humpf

Sizzli

Uh UUH! **I** don't mark up my body either. I hate needles.

Then Sasha turns Sizzli around in front of the mirror and low and behold on her left shoulder is R/S .

NNEEEAAT. I wonder how that got there. I'll bet that'll get me a few extra dollars tonight.

Sasha

A few extra dollars? What **exactly** is it that you do here? Humpf

Sizzli

I'm a dancer. You got a problem with that?

Sasha

Oh no! Not at all! I love to dance. Waltz, Tango, Cha Cha, Two Step, Morange' **(She shakes her head from left to right singing)**

Sasha cont..

aaaand to the left side…ttthhheeenn to the right side… aaaand to the left side…ttthhheeenn to the right side… humpf)

Sizzli

No fool! I'm an exotic dancer.

Sasha

Exotic? Exotic like the Mediterranean? Oh I like you already.

Sizzli

Look, let me try to explain. I'll talk sssllllooow so you can understand. Better yet, I'll show you.

(**Sizzli moves up close to Sasha and puts her right hand on Sasha's left shoulder and the other was just straight down like she was keeping her balance.**)

Sizzli

Now you put your right hand on my left shoulder and I'll show you how it's done.

(**Sasha was hesitant but she put her right hand on Sizzli's left shoulder. If anybody was looking down from the ceiling, it'd look like a human "O".**)

Narrator: Just as Sasha placed her right hand on Sizzli's left shoulder, the strangest thing happened...

Sasha

OK, this is really fun but what's the point? Humpf

Sizzli

Nevermind. Let's go back to the lobby. Customers should be coming soon.

Narrator: So out of the tiny piece of a dressing room they went. But wait a minute. Something is wrong. They aren't on the Eastside anymore. Where are they now?

(The ladies take two steps into what looks like very big room with expensive furniture, paintings on the wall, marble floors a fire place, chandelier lighting. In the middle of the room, standing as if suspended is something that looks like a cane. No a crutch with wings at the bottom.)

Narrator cont. *Well what have we here and what do you know, it's The Strangest Thing (Ah chew – I sneezed) Yes you're right - a* **PogoStick***. I didn't write this part either.*

Sasha

Now **this** is more like it. Looks like somewhere that I would live. Funny, it didn't look like this when I came in here. Sizzli, how'd you do that?

Sizzli

Will you just shut up. I remember being in the dressing closet, I remember you changing your dress, I remember me changing my shirt. I remember us going back to the lobby. OK! **(She screams) What's going on!!**

Narrator: *It's right there silly women. Give it a second just wait, this is really The Strangest Thing (Ah chew – I sneezed). They hear a voice from that thing in middle of the floor.*

The Strangest Thing

Ladies, ladies. Let me introduce myself –

Sasha

Who said that?

Sizzli *(saying loudly)*

Ms. Thang, Mr. Thang. Come on yawl jokes over. This isn't funny.

Narrator: That pogo stick that I told you about – well it talks. It does some other things too believe me. It really is The Strangest Thing – (Ahchew I sneezed)

The Strangest Thing

Ladies, I know you're a little thrown off but this will be a new endeavor for the two of you. **I** am The Strangest Thing.

Sasha

You sure are.

Sizzli

Yeah yeah the strangest thing. What's your name?

The Strangest Thing

That's my name. Remember Ganna was trying to tell you that she saw me.

Sizzli

Well I'll be. Ganna did say that she saw the strangest thing. I thought she'd just missed a meal.

Sasha

Wow. Is this your place? You seen Lady? What **is** her name?

The Strangest Thing

Actually ladies, this is **your** Palace. I've been just waiting for the right moment to let you see. Now here's the thing. You both are Swintons.

Sasha says to Sizzli

Waite a minute! Your name is Swinton too. Why didn't you say something?

Sizzli

Because **you** have issues! You never ask and I would never believe that we were even related.

The Strangest Thing

Like I was saying. Here's the thing. Your pappa was a rolling stone. Rich. Like rolling in dough. Sasha how do you think you came upon all that bread?

Narrator: *You think he went a little too far with that?*

The Strangest Thing

Sasha, your father met your mother in Scotland. They fell in love, never got married, but you were the product of their love. Sizzli, your father met your mother in America and you were the product of their passion. He couldn't keep the two of you together but he did make arrangements for the two of you to meet each other, find your relatives and share the wealth.

Sasha

You mean, this palace is ours? The money too? I can get another Benz? More diamonds? More silks? **(rubbing her hands together)** Wait – we have relatives??

Sizzli

Sasha – shut up. All you do is wyne and complain. Wyne and complain.

Narrator: Sounds like a terrible song. It not as bad as: aaaand to the left side...ttthhheeenn to the right side... aaaand to the left side...ttthhheeenn to the right side.

Sizzli (cont.)

This is fine and dandy but I know there's a catch, what is it?

The Strangest Thing

Glad you ask. You'll probably meet Fine and Dandy another time. Here's the thing, you're father was a traveling man and he was really handsome so he had no problem with the ladies......

Sasha

I know. I got my looks from my daaaaaddy. That's what my mommy said. Humpf!

Sizzli

Your mommy should have told you to shut up sometimes. Go on

Narrator: *Now you've got two ladies talking to a pogo stick. The really strange part is that's it's an intelligent conversation and his answers aren't bouncing all over the place...*

The Strangest Thing

He was also a triplet. Two boys and one girl. Because of a family dispute they separated. Moving to different parts of the world.

After years of the misery with the left hand not knowing what the right hand is doing, your father made me to be a combination of the strength of metal, to keep the family together, handles to make sure you get a grip and a pogostick body that he hoped would be something to stop attitudes from bouncing up and down and the narrow wings down bottom. I'm not sure what they're for. **(turning to the side and back)** You think they make me took too skinny? His next thing was how to bring the family together.

He dabbled a little into magic so he made the medallions with R/S in the middle. When you touch it, it shatters but the R/S transfers to your left shoulder. What happens then is when a Royal Swinton touches the left shoulder of another Royal Swinton with their right hand, it removed your troubles and brings you home. Here to the Palace.

Sizzli

My world was just fine until this *woman* showed up. Looks to me like my troubles have just begun. So let me get this straight. I've got to locate some people that I don't know, don't even care about, give them a hug and share all this? Shoot, it's bad enough that I've run across a complete idiot only to find out that she's my sister, then I get taken away from my home without my permission for some alternate reality and given instructions from a stick thing and I'm supposed to go for it. I'll take the palace but can't you find my father the magician and make her disappear.

Sasha (shaking her head in confusion)

Waite a minute Sizzli. It's the Strangest Thing and he may be onto something but I guess you wouldn't know since you're obviously from the deprived- I mean less fortunate side of the family. You wouldn't know a good thing if it ran you over. Humpf. How does this work again?

The Strangest Thing

Well if you remember the notes where it says – find the others. Well, the others is more than a bar.

Narrator: Sorry Sizzli

The Strangest Thing

I meant the other members of your family. You find them, touch the left shoulder with the right hand. The right hand knows what the left side is doing and you come home. To the Palace

Sasha

Like an "O"

The Strangest Thing

That's right. An "O" for OTHERS. Plus it's really a hug. Your father knew that there may be some distance with family so it's the closest thing to a hug. Your mission, and you have no choice but to except it, is to find the other Swintons and bring them home to the Palace.

Sizzli

Tell me something. Why is it that every time somebody says your name they sneeze?

The Strangest Thing

Good question. Here's the thing. See your father kept a cold so when he sneezed I told him that it looked like the strangest thing so that's what he named me – The Strangest Thing. OK he had jokes.

But he did say that I was a blessing so he has delegated one person to see me and let the Swinton know about me. When that person says my name, it's a blessing to the Swinton's so.....

Sizzli

Well now isn't that just special. He should have named you that.

Sasha

As tired as I was just trying to find "The Others", how are we supposed to travel all the way around the world to find relatives that we don't even know?

The Strangest Thing

Here's the thing. Like I said, you get to the palace just like you got here. You just have to place your right hand on the left shoulder of your sister. Once you get to the palace, to go to another city or state, put me in the middle, get a grip, pound me on the ground two times and just say any country and you're there. The Swinton will find you.

You can't miss a Swinton cause when the time is right for them, they will have been told about me, found the medallion, which will transfer the R/S on their left shoulders. Once they've found you, just make that circle and you will be right here at the Palace.

Sasha

You mean I get to travel for free? It's better than accumulating free air miles…..

Sizzli

Sasha – SHUT UPPPPPP!! So that's how we got the tattoo. Nice! OK so what happens if we don't find any more Swintons?

The Strangest Thing

They're around. All over the country. You've just got to look. Don't worry, where ever you go, they will find you.

Sizzli

How come we don't sneeze when we say your name?

The Strangest Thing

Because I was the blessing specially made for you. They sneeze, and you say bless you and that's it. The only person who will see me is the friend of the Swinton. They see me, I have them tell you about me then you find the medallion. When you hear someone sneeze, your family is somewhere near.

Narrator: Waite a minute, I'm the one telling the story so I sneeze all the time. Nobody ever says bless you.   Do I get a palace? No! I just get to tell this story. OK at least I've got a job.

Sasha

AALLRRIIGHTY!   Let's try this thingy out.   Now tell me again, how it works?

The Strangest Thing

Just put your right hand on Sizzli's left shoulder, put me in the middle, get a grip, call out a country, bounce me twice and you're there.   Just know that once you have gotten to your destination, when you loose your grip, you won't see me again until you get back to the Palace.   Got It?

Sizzli

OK Sasha, put your hand on my shoulder, I'll do the same and let's get a grip.

(They bounce The Strangest Thing two times and say two different countries.)

The Strangest Thing

You might want to decide which country you want to go to before you bounce me. I'm not going to be young forever – Please be gentle.

Sasha

I want to go to Paris!

Sizzli

You've probably already been there and I'm sure Paris is happy that you're not there anymore.

The Strangest Thing

I'll tell you what. I'll choose this first place. After that, you're on your own.

(The Strangest Thing bounces two times and Sasha and Sizzli end up in another Country. They hit the ground, loose their grip, drop The Strangest Thing and it's gone.)

Sasha

Now that was interesting. Ask us where we're goin'. We don't know....

Narrator: Well this is how the story begins. You've got two women that didn't know they were sisters until just an hour ago. They've got family all over the world that they probably won't know at first glance. They've been given instructions from a talking POGOSTICK that stands alone. Now isn't that just the strangest thing - ah chew (I sneezed)

THE ROYAL SWINTONS
R/S